The Man Who Murdered His Muse

James Champagne

The Man Who Murdered His Muse

by James Champagne

ISBN: 978-1-908125-73-6

Cover Art by David Rix

Publication Date: March 2019

All text copyright 2019 James Champagne

"A work of Genius is a Work 'Not to be obtain'd
by the Invocation of Memory & her Syren Daughters
but by Devout prayer to that Eternal Spirit, who can
enrich with all utterance & knowledge & sends out his
Seraphim with the hallowed fire of his Altar to touch
& purify the lips of whom he pleases."

-John Milton, *The Reason of Church Government*

When I first informed Father that I had landed a part-time job tending bar for the weekends, you would have thought I had told him that we had just won the lottery, the way his face lit up. "You're not going to regret this, Hamsa," he had said. "Trust me, as a bartender, you'll get so much material for stories it won't even be funny. Get ready to kiss your writer's block goodbye." My father (a retired electrical engineer who once upon a time worked for the Cosmodemonic Telegraph Company of North America, and who also suffered from a minor affliction of acromegaly) was of the unshakeable belief that bartenders, because of the nature of their job (what with their being regularly exposed to random strangers, much like taxi drivers in that regard), were continually bombarded with potential grist for the old literary mill. Of course, Father was a firm believer in a great many oddball theories, most of which turned out to be total bullshit. Like how the planet Earth was not shaped like a globe, but rather a lemniscate. Or that the human race constituted the fifth in a series of primordial root-races (to this day, my father is still the only person I've ever known who has read every single last word in H.P. Blavatsky's mind-numbingly boring esoteric tome *The Secret*

Doctrine … multiple times!). Or that he had it in him to translate the notorious Voynich Manuscript (a task that he toiled away at in his spare time for many years). Or (most improbably of all) that George R.R. Martin would finish writing *The Winds of Winter*, the sixth book of his A Song of Ice and Fire series, before the sixth season of *Game of Thrones* aired.

In light of my father's poor track record with pet theories, perhaps I should have been more skeptical of his supposal that working bartender at a night club would be a great way to meet a host of diverse and interesting strangers. But truth be told this was something that I myself wanted to believe: I would even fantasize that working at the bar would allow me to meet a legion of bizarre personalities straight out of the lyrics of a Lou Reed song (with hardboiled noir nicknames attached, much like the No Wave New Yorkers who gravitated towards such urban monikers in the late 1970's and early 1980's), each with a fascinating life story to tell. But it only took a few shifts working bar at the night club in question to shatter all of my illusions in that regard. Why mince words? One lonely drunk is a lot like any other lonely drunk, and most of them had identical life sob stories: fired from their dead-end job, living with their parents, lost custody of their kids to their ex-spouse, couldn't find love, lost all faith in God, boo fucking hoo.

My name is Hamsa Cauldron. At the time of which I'm writing about, I was a freshman student at a New England university in the City. This university is a small and private liberal arts college that boasted a student body of around 600. Despite the fact that this student body was mostly made up of pretentious occult-obsessed art students, and that the faculty consisted of equally pretentious (and extremely lecherous) professors, I suppose it was a nice enough place to go to school. The campus was quite scenic, and the City itself was a pretty cool town, full of quaint-looking examples of colonial architecture, some beautiful (and very old) churches, and a great number of antiquarian bookstores. As a budding bibliophile, I was drawn to these antiquarian bookstores like a gazelle to a watering hole, and in our free time my roommate (a fellow bibliophile who went by the name of Dinah) and I enjoyed haunting such establishments.

The problem that I very quickly ran into was that old books can often be somewhat pricey (especially the types of books I gravitated towards), and money was something that I was often in short supply of. So after a few weeks into my freshman year, in early October 2016, I decided to get a weekend job. A flyer tacked up to the poster board hanging on the wall of the campus' coffee house informed me that Hollow Hills, the City's sole Goth club, was seeking bartenders to work evenings on the weekend, which was exactly what I was looking for. I was surprised that the City even had a Goth club in the first place, as I had presumed that such establishments had long vanished into extinction. Being something of a Goth myself (indeed, the university did seem to attract a large number of Goth students in general), landing the job proved to be a piece of cake. And that explains how I found myself working as a bartender (though as I was under 21 years of age, I couldn't legally drink the stuff I was serving, which was no big deal as when it comes to liquid refreshment I prefer plain old water anyway).

Hollow Hills (so named after the classic 1981 Bauhaus single) was located in one of the less scenic neighborhoods of the City. Despite its seedy location (it was situated directly across the street from a cemetery, another popular hangout for the local Goths), the place itself was relatively upscale, as far as Goth clubs went. Black was, as to be expected, the primary color: the walls, floors and ceilings of the club were thus completely covered in black paint, almost as if the very night itself had slithered into the establishment and splayed itself out within the architectural dimensions. Not that black was the only color: the windows at the front of the club were decorated with purple lace curtains, red electric candles (placed in elaborate gilt candelabras) provided illumination, and over the dance floor large red and green beams of light sliced the darkness into jagged shapes, as if a duel were taking place in the air between a number of titanic (and invisible) Jedi Masters and Sith Lords. Framed art prints (displaying the cover art of such classic Goth albums as *In The Flat Field* by Bauhaus, *Juju* by Siouxsie & the Banshees, and *Pornography* by The Cure) adorned many of the club's walls, and papering the space in-between these frames were flyers advertising gigs for local rock bands (nearly all of whom sported such 'mature' nicknames as Sucking Chest Wound). The club's house DJ was an S&M mask-wearing freak known only as DJ Lautréamont (who had been something of a big name in the club scene down in Miami back in the 1980's), and every evening he played a great selection of goth, post-punk, industrial and darkwave music from the 70's, 80's and 90's. All in all, it was a pretty sweet place to work, and my co-workers were for the most part cool people that I enjoyed hanging out with.

Would that I could say the same about the clientele. As I noted at the onset of this narrative, most of the people I served booze to weren't the most interesting individuals that I've happened to come across. There was, however, one exception: Hector Teufel. The evening when I first made his acquaintance certainly remains etched in my mind. It was sometime in mid-November, and by that point in time I had been working at Hollow Hills for around a month or so. It was on a Sunday evening, and the place was pretty empty, perhaps on account of the dismal weather: the sky wasn't just raining cats and dogs, it was pissing Anomalous

Big Cats and Black Dogs (or Black Shucks, for those readers who might hail from the East Anglia region). There were a small handful of people on the dance floor, and from my vantage point behind the bar I could analyze from a distance the subcultural zoology on display. There were some specimens of the typical university art student variety (easy to identify as 90% of them sported *Eraserhead* or *A Clockwork Orange* t-shirts), shirtless dudes wearing black leather pants and gimp masks, and a number of Goths: fragile-looking teens with pale porcelain-white skin and dyed black hair, clad in black antique dresses (mainly the girls in that regard, though a few of the boys as well) and fishnet. The tenebrous kohl smeared haphazardly around the upper hemispheres of their faces made it look as if their eyes were white spaceships caught in the act of being consumed by miniature black holes. Many of these teens wore hesitation marks and faux-suicide scars on their wrists like twilight tattoos or shadow sigils: biological hieroglyphs detailing a personal monomyth of a private pain made public. DJ Lautréamont was behind his console in the DJ booth spinning tunes, and most of the people assembled on the dance floor were (unsurprisingly) dancing to the music he had pounding out over the club's sound system, which at that current moment was 'Monsters' by The Crüxshadows (specifically the v2.0 version of the song as taken from their 2001 compilation album *Echoes and Artifacts*). I myself was a huge

Crüxshadows fan, especially their first two albums, their underrated 1993 debut *…Night Crawls In* and 1995's *Telemetry of a Fallen Angel.*

The bar in particular was quiet that evening, which gave me a lot of free time to pursue my other interests. I tried reading a few pages of William Hope Hodgson's *The Night Land* (itself a reading assignment for one of my Lit courses), but with the loud and pounding music I was unable to focus on the florid content. Eventually I just put the book back down on a shelf under the counter of the bar and spent my idle time checking my cellphone for any texts from Samantha, my girlfriend. Thinking about Samantha naturally got me horny, and I ended up picturing myself in a dildo-laden threesome with Helen Marnie and Mira Aroyo from *Velocifero*-era Ladytron.

My Ladytron erotic daydream was just getting good when I noticed a customer approaching the bar, just as DJ Lautréamont began playing The Fall's 'New Face in Hell'. I had never laid eyes on this stranger before, and he seemed out of place in this environment: he looked more like the kind of man who would be more comfortable playing the word 'tetrasporic' at a Scrabble championship tournament than hanging out at a Goth club. He was a middle-aged man in a ratty black suit, and in terms of physical appearance he looked almost exactly like Leonora Carrington's eerie 1943 sfumato drawing of Dr. Luis Morales, the creepy Santander psychiatrist who she had depicted as Dr. Don Luis Morales in her memoir *Down Below*, which was to say that his face was round, clean-shaven and almost like that of a babe (and by babe I mean a Babe of the Abyss), with pursed lips, a receding black hairline that terminated as a widow's peak on his forehead, and very large and sinister eyes, eyes that were a shade of White Walker blue and which seemed almost too large for his face. An existential darkness floated in those eyes like two plague ships plowing through the vitreous oceans of dyadic parallel universes, and an expression of profound uneasiness marred his somewhat childlike features, as if a Burroughsian Death Dwarf had burrowed into his skull and contaminated his thoughts with its own disturbing dreams.

As he took a seat at the bar and I sized him up, I wondered what he thought about when he looked at me: a short and thin 19 year-old black lesbian (for the record, I've often been told that I bear a strong resemblance to the actress Cherie Johnson during her *Family Matters* days: while on the subject, I'll never understand why Steve Urkel was so hot for Laura when it was fairly obvious that Maxine was way cuter, but I digress) with short dark brown hair. Let's see, whatever was I wearing that evening? … ah yes, I believe I was wearing a white short-sleeved t-shirt, on the front of which was an illustration of the face of a one-eyed cyclops girl with long brown hair and no nose, executed in an abstract 1980's style (Dustin Diamond wore an identical-looking t-shirt as his Screech Powers character from the *Saved by the Bell* episode known as 'Blind Date', so obviously I was making some kind of retro-ironic hipster fashion statement that evening), along with tight black leather pants and scruffy black Dr. Martens boots.

After I made him his drink (absinthe was his poison of choice … how pretentious), we engaged in a bit of casual conversation. "So, what do you do?" the stranger asked, once I had served him his drink.

"I'm a student over here at the university," I replied.

"Oh yes? Good school, from what I hear, though I'm a Rhode Island College alumni myself … class of '83," the man said as he nursed his drink. He had a slight South American accent. "So what are you studying, if you don't mind my asking?"

"No, I don't mind," I said with a shrug. "I'm majoring in Hauntology, with a minor in Creative Writing."

"Creative writing, you say? Interesting, very interesting," the stranger murmured.

"So what do you do?" I asked him, as I rested an elbow on the glowing counter of the bar.

"Well, I suppose you could say that I'm a man of letters," the stranger drawled. He took a sip of his drink, and then asked, "Tell me, does the name Hector Teufel mean anything to you?"

"To be honest, not really, though it certainly *sounds* familiar in a manner I can't place," I answered back.

"It doesn't surprise me that you don't know who I am … you're obviously young, and my prime was before your time," the man said. "I'm a writer, you see. Or, to be more exact, I *was* a writer. These days I'm just your garden variety professional alcoholic."

"Oh yeah?" I asked, mildly interested now. "What kind of stuff did you write? Like poetry for magazines and that kind of thing?"

And here the stranger gave me a Delphian smile, showing all of his teeth. His smile made me very uncomfortable: it was like the blade of a tiny sickle cutting through the comforting shadows of the club. In contrast to his somewhat down-on-his-luck vibe, his teeth were Joel Osteen-immaculate. I've never been able to trust people whose teeth look that nice: people with a smile so emblematic of perfection are usually hiding something, or overcompensating to cover up some sinister character defect. The man went on to say, "Oh, nothing as commonplace as that, my dear, I was no mere scribbler … believe it or not but I was actually a bigshot bestselling author back in the 1980's."

I raised an eyebrow skeptically. "Really? If you were such a bestselling author, what are you doing here at Hollow Hills on a Sunday night?"

"Because where does a fallen angel go after their fall from grace?" Mr. Teufel asked in a rhetorical manner. "The only place they can go … *down*."

Now he had really captivated my attention, and I began to entertain the notion that I had finally made the acquaintance of an interesting barfly: what if he was telling the truth and he literally *was* a fallen angel? Granted, it didn't seem likely, but stranger things have happened. "So, what were some of the books you wrote?" I asked, mainly to keep him talking.

"Ever heard of a little book named *Whim*?" Mr. Teufel asked.

Now *that* jogged some memories. I realized that Mr. Teufel was making a jest, for there was nothing little about *Whim*: it was one of those bulky doorstopper horror novels that were so popular back in the 1980's, a book that was over a thousand pages long. Father had been a fan of the book, and I recalled memories of seeing him reading it when I was a child, and how he had described the plotline to me. The front cover had depicted a painting of a small town that looked like something out of a 1950's Norman Rockwell illustration, with the word 'Whim' in bloody red capital letters in the sky above, the blood dripping down onto the houses and people below. Like most 80's horror novels the plot was the usual nonsense: something about a small town named Thundermist in Rhode Island being invaded by some kind of mysterious alien force that took control of people's bodies and forced them to carry out their most debased whims.

"So you wrote *Whim*?" I asked, impressed.

"Along with a number of other bestselling horror novels and short story collections, though the novels always sold better," Mr. Teufel said. He then began regaling me with a long and rambling story of the rise and fall of his career as a bestselling novelist. As he related to me, the 1980's was a very lucrative period in time for the horror fiction industry, what with the success of writers such as Stephen King, Peter Straub and Dean Koontz (among many others: even that talentless hack Richard Madoc had found success with books like *…And my Love*), and upon graduating college, Mr. Teufel had wanted in on the ground floor. Though as he admitted to me, this hadn't been as easy as he initially thought it would be.

"What do you mean?" I asked.

"It was my greatest desire to be a writer … a man of letters. I was possessed by the dream that so many of us pursue with all the zeal of Ponce de León seeking the Fountain of Youth: to walk into a bookstore and see a book with one's name on the front cover. My problem was that while I wanted to be a writer, I was unable to come up with any interesting ideas. I lacked that most crucial of creative conspirators: a muse."

"So let me guess: you got your hands on a Trichinobezoar extracted from some hapless lass' stomach (no doubt suffering from Rapunzel Syndrome) and pawned it off to some grotty occultist in exchange for a poor captive Calliope?" I asked sardonically.

"You've been reading too much Gaiman, girl," Mr. Teufel said as he folded his hands together, thus causing them to look like a briar patch of fingers, or perhaps the logo of some particularly pretentious Norwegian death metal band. "What can one do when not blessed with the patronage of a muse? One simply fashions one himself. In college I had once read a book on Tibetan Mysticism, and there had been a chapter on how to create servitors, thought-forms … the technical name for such things are tulpas, though a Western occultist would classify them as egregores. The way it works is that you make these beings with your mind and then they take on a life of their own. So that's what I ended up doing. And believe you me, it was no simple task. But in the end, I created my very own muse. But during the alchemical process, something went awry and it came out … wrong."

And here Mr. Teufel took a few moments to describe the physical appearance of his misbegotten muse. In spite of my usually excellent memory, I find that for this section of our conversation I have forgotten the exact words he used, but my general impression of the anatomical characteristics of the beast brought to mind the bizarre and phallic-looking ape/bear hybrid creature that graces the front cover art of Fleetwood Mac's 1973 album

Mystery to Me: that book-devouring beast whose lips were smeared with dripping cake frosting. Upon the termination of his discourse on the creation of the monstrous muse, I asked him, "Okay, so you had your muse. What then?"

"You know, it's a funny thing … although I took the creation of my muse quite seriously, at the same time there was a small part of me that didn't really believe it would work," Mr. Teufel said, a haunted look in his eyes now. I noted that for a guy who had just finished drinking a glass of absinthe, he seemed remarkably sober. "And yet it *did* work. Shortly after my muse began taking on a life of its own, ideas began to blossom within the barren fields of my imagination. These ideas eventually mutated into the project that became my first novel: *The Dark Project*. I was quite surprised that I actually finished the damn thing, and was shocked when it got published and went on to become an international bestseller. And just like that, I was in the big time."

It was at this point in our conversation that Mr. Teufel's narrative became a condensed summary of his life as a big-shot horror writer living in Manhattan in the 1980's. I listened with rapt attention, for his reminisces were as intoxicating to me as were Arthur Machen's childhood memories of seeing the faery dome above the pimpled summit of Twmbarlwm in South Wales. In some ways it was almost like listening to an audio book adaptation of a Bret Easton Ellis novel, only this was real life, and as Mr. Teufel unspooled his narrative it was as if the Goth music that formed the acoustical background ambience of the club faded away and was replaced with Peter Gabriel's 'Big Time' (a song that he recalled was playing over the radio inside a limousine that had escorted him to a book launch party in Manhattan one evening back in 1986: during the ride up he had snorted lines of cocaine off some escort girl's bare leg). His narrative here became a confused whirl of hedonistic parties, debauches at clubs like Tunnel and the Palladium, hobnobbing with Bret Easton Ellis and Jay McInerney and Tama Janowitz and the rest of the literary Brat Pack, and power lunches with publishers at Mortimer's. This had all culminated with the publication of his epic horror novel *Whim* in 1988 or so: like all of his previous books, this one had also been a bestseller.

"My last bestseller, sadly," Mr. Teufel said, as he reached the end of this portion of his tale.

"So what happened next?"

Mr. Teufel sighed. "What I had wasn't enough. I was dissatisfied with my work. Sure, I was a bestselling author, but at the same time no one really respected me: all of the prominent literary critics of the day treated me like a joke. After a while I was sick of being their metaphysical punching bag. I didn't want to be known as a mere writer of penny dreadfuls. I wanted to write something that would demonstrate my range as an artist, I wanted to pen a true blue literary novel.

My only problem was my muse … my monster of a muse. Such a creature was useful for one and only one purpose: the inspiration of works of horror. After some meditation, my path became clear … the only solution was to murder my muse and replace it with something more powerful."

"But how do you go about murdering an imaginary being?" I asked, raising an eyebrow.

"Isn't it obvious? With an imaginary gun, to quote an old issue from Grant Morrison's *Doom Patrol* run," Mr. Teufel said with a mysterious smile, a smile I found as esoteric as the black and white photograph of Catherine Robbe-Grillet that Roger Viollet took of her at her home in Neuilly-sur-Seine in 1985. "In any event, that's just what I did … which I suppose makes me the man who murdered his muse."

"Which would also make you the first murderer that I've ever served beer to," I remarked.

"Careful now, you speak more truthfully than you know. But allow me to let you in on a little trade secret. All writers are fairy slayers and murderers of the imagination. People like us go on safaris within the wilderness in our heads and we collect ideas as if they were exotic butterflies. We pluck these things right out of thin air and pin them to the page. A book is not a hymn to the living, but a necropolis of dead dreams," Mr. Teufel said. "Now, you seem like an intelligent girl. Have you perchance ever heard of E.M. Cioran?"

20

"The name certainly rings a bell," I said, thinking about it. "I don't believe that I've ever read any of his books, but now that you mention it, I recall that Hideo Kojima quoted him in the most recent *Metal Gear Solid* game."

"A number of years ago I happened across an interview with Cioran and he had this one quotation that obsessed me to such a degree that I eventually memorized it by heart: 'As soon as one has written something down, it loses its secret at once, it gets lost, is killed: one has 'killed' the thing and oneself. But writing has precisely this function. I have noticed, by the way, that those who do not write have more resources, because they store up everything within themselves. To have written something down means to have dragged it out of oneself, to have uttered definitively everything that came from inside. A writer is someone who gives away that which is most original to him, finally losing, in this manner, his whole substance. That is why writers are so uninteresting as a rule and I mean that quite seriously: writers are people who have exhausted themselves. Only the dregs of themselves still exist; they are pitiful marionettes.'" Mr. Teufel paused his narrative to light a cigarette. He took a long drag off it, then continued. "Do you want to know the problem with the writers of your generation? So many of them have no interest in writing literature. No, they're waging a crusade, carrying out a social mission. It's like one big popularity contest … they want to be 'liked' by everyone, seen as good people, on the right side of history and all that tosh. But for fuck's sake, we aren't writing Sunday sermons here, it's not our job to compose instruction manuals for morality or empowerment self-help pamphlets. Maybe Victor Hugo or Dostoyevsky could get away with such a thing, but let me tell you, your generation has yet to put forth its own Hugo or Dostoyevsky … but fuck it, it's not like my generation ever did, either. To me, the main attraction for writing fiction in the first place was that it seemed to be an invitation to engage in imaginary acts of immorality … or if that word offends your liberal sensibilities, maybe amorality would do. We like to think of ourselves as angels, but when push comes to shove we find ourselves doing the Devil's work. None of us are all that good … everyone is guilty."

I was suddenly aware that Mr. Teufel's speech was rapidly turning into a lecture. Trying to steer him back on course, I said "So, you murdered your muse."

"Yes, there I was, a man without a muse. Once again I had succeeded at a seemingly impossible task. But you know what Oscar Wilde once wrote about the gods … when they wish to torture us, they simply answer our prayers. There's a lot of truth contained in that old chestnut, let me tell you. Once I was free of my muse, I began my grand attempt to write my Great American Novel. It didn't take me long to realize that I really *wasn't* the kind of writer capable of creating such a thing

… that I wasn't a literary writer at all. Soon enough I began to miss my muse, began to miss writing those horror novels and short stories that had once given me such joy. So one day in the early 1990's I began trying to lure my old muse back."

"But how would that even be possible?" I asked, confused. "You told me that you had murdered your muse, remember?"

"In theory, on an abstract level, yes, of course, but as Alan Moore observed in his comic book *V for Vendetta*, ideas are bulletproof," Mr. Teufel said (I had, by this point, come to the conclusion that the man was something of a comic book buff). "It was just a simple matter of restoring my muse to life and coaxing it to come back to me. But I soon came to learn that muses can be … fickle. They don't bestow their gifts on just anyone, and when they do, it is a gift not given away lightly. To then go and reject their patronage, well … perhaps in their eyes such an action is unforgiveable. Anyway, my old muse apparently now found me unworthy. And I did try my hardest to lure it back, but to no avail."

"What do you mean by 'luring it back?'"

"What's the best way to attract the favors of a monster? By performing monstrous acts of one's own, by becoming a monster oneself. It was to that end that I began to immerse myself into a life of crime." Mr. Teufel said this so casually one could have been mistaken for thinking he was discussing the latest dress worn by Beyoncé at some film premiere. "I started off with small offenses at first, such as thievery, then began working my way up to major crimes, the sort of atrocities that would have made even the divine Marquis De Sade blush at the merest thought of them. Not only did I take part in the Black Mass and other acts of blasphemy, I also indulged in torture, rape, necrophilia … and murder."

"Murder, you say," I said, trying to smother a yawn. I was unsure if the man standing before me on the other side of the bar was telling the truth now, or if the absinthe he had imbibed earlier had finally caught up to him and was now inspiring him to proclaim all sorts of nonsense. "So tell me, what was the worst crime you ever committed?"

"Ah, but there are so many potential candidates for that particular honor," Mr. Teufel said with a sinister smile, once again making an atrocity exhibition of those immaculate teeth. "There was the time I broke into that mausoleum and had sex with bloated, maggot-ridden corpses. Or that little Jewish girl I kidnapped, stripped naked, and raped on H.P. Lovecraft's grave one Halloween night: during the act I forced her to wear an extremely realistic-looking Anne Frank mask over her face, so that it made it seem as if I were raping Anne Frank. But as for the very worse crime, well –"

"I think I get the idea," I said, holding up a hand to indicate I wasn't interested in hearing anymore. I was once again aware of the music that

DJ Lautréamont was playing at that moment, the song being 'Undone' by Bauhaus. "So, despite all these horrible things you did, you weren't able to lure your old muse back, right?"

"Indeed, it was all for naught," Mr. Teufel said as he stubbed the remnants of his cigarette out in a nearby ashtray (which was shaped like an upside-down pentagram). "No matter what I did, no matter what I tried, my muse never returned to me. By the year 2000, after a decade of debauchery and decadence, I realized that it was never coming back and I just gave up the ghost, metaphorically speaking. And so I've spent the last 16 years or so drifting from place to place, never staying in one spot for long, slowly drinking myself to an early grave … and now here I am, in this godforsaken city."

And here the former writer lapsed into a gloomy silence. Not sure what else to say to him, I decided to proffer some advice. "Okay, look, I'll play along," I said. "Hypothetically, let's say that everything that you told me here tonight is true. Maybe your mistake is trying to cling to your old muse. And maybe your solution is to just find a new one. To reinvent yourself, like David Bowie or Lady Gaga. To rise like a phoenix from the ashes of your old life."

Mr. Teufel considered my advice for a few quiet moments, a thoughtful expression on his baby's face. "You know, you just might be onto something," he eventually said. "I'll have to let that advice sink in and see how I feel about it in the morning. As things stand, I've wasted enough of your night prattling away like an old biddy, obnubilating your pretty little head with darkness and shadows. The night beckons me, and I must now be on my way. Goodbye, my dear, and best of luck in your own writing endeavors." He was just about to get up from his seat, but something stopped him at the last moment. "Ah, how embarrassing, we've been talking all this time and I've never caught your name."

"Hamsa Cauldron," I answered, feeling no real desire to lie to him, in spite of his creeper vibe.

"Hamsa Cauldron … what a lovely name. Well, it was nice to meet you, Hamsa." And with those words spoken, Hector Teufel rose from his stool at the bar and beat a hasty retreat for the exit. A few seconds later and he had vacated the premises entirely.

"What a weirdo," I muttered to myself. Still, it had been a very interesting conversation, even though I found much of what he said hard to swallow. I thought that I'd never see him again. But it turned out that I was wrong, for in truth the span of time separating my first meeting with him to my second was as short-lived as the life cycle of an ephemeron.

Flash forward to a late afternoon in early May, towards the end of the spring semester. I was in my dorm room at Karswell Hall, hanging out with my roommate (and fellow bibliophile) Dinah. We had just gotten high and were listening to the song 'The Finest Drops' off the 1988 Wire album *A Bell Is a Cup … Until It Is Struck* (one of their better tunes, in my opinion, though that whole album is really worth listening to). Dinah was resting on her bed in her half of the room we shared, and she was nodding her head in time to the music while flipping through Philip Best's book *Alien Existence*. I was seated at my desk (and before my computer) in my half of the room, staring at a blank Microsoft Word document, the cursor winking in and out of existence at the upper west (or left hand) corner of the page. It was a Friday night, and I had a short story assignment to complete for my creative writing class the following Monday. But my writer's block was as bad as it had ever been, and I couldn't think of a single idea worth setting down on paper. I was unable to think of anything but the city of Dis as described by Dante in the sixth circle of his *Inferno*: a walled city for the souls of active sinners, its gates guarded by gorgons and fallen angels. I forget if Dante described where exactly the city's main gate was, but in my opinion the most likely place was undoubtedly on the upper west corner of the great wall, and I cursed that particular spatial direction. Feeling desperate, I glanced over to the side of my computer monitor, where standing sentinel on the desk was a Funko Samuel R. Delany POP figurine, and as I gazed into the soulless round black eyes of this simulacra of my favorite writer, I prayed for a divine lightning bolt of inspiration to pass between us, but sadly, such a communion never transpired.

"So how's the story going?" Dinah eventually asked me, still nodding her head to the music.

I tried to think of a witty response, but was just too disgusted with myself to even put up such an effort. "Like shit," I groaned, as I closed the Word document and shut down my computer. "Fuck it, I think I'm gonna head out."

"What are your plans?" Dinah asked, as she placed her book down on the bed next to her.

"Seeing as how most of the antiquarian bookstores we usually hit are closed at this hour, I was thinking of maybe going to Covers," I said.

"Really? That might not be such a good idea today."

"Oh? Why not?"

"You mean you haven't heard? Some prominent author is going to be there this afternoon and evening, doing a signing for his new book."

"Who's the writer?"

"Oh man, he had a strange name ... they had a story about it in the newspaper this morning.

Hector something or other," Dinah said, her red-rimmed eyes squinted in thought.

I then felt a curious tingling feeling going up and down my back, as if my spinal vertebrae were being caressed by the Disembodied Hand That Strangled People (as dreamed up by Calvin's father in the *Calvin & Hobbes* cartoon strip). "Was his name Hector Teufel, perhaps?" I asked, even though I already knew what the answer would be.

"Indeed it was. Did you read the story as well, Hamsa?"

"No, just a lucky guess on my part," I said in an airy tone that belied my true feelings. "This book that he's come out with, do you perchance remember what the title was?"

"Yes, that I do remember: it was something like *Jacob's Triumph*," Dinah said, visibly perking up. "Some kind of feel-good Christian fiction novel … you know, like *The Shack*."

Now *that* really was a surprise. After my initial (and to date only) encounter with Hector Teufel the previous year, I hadn't really expected him to ever take up writing again, and, on the off chance that he did, I had always assumed it would be a return to the horror genre. But now he had apparently transformed himself into a writer of Christian Fiction, of all things? I then made up my mind that I would pay a visit to the Covers bookstore and find out just what had happened to him. I wasn't really looking forward to this reunion, but my sense of curiosity overruled my better judgment. Luckily, I just so happened to have one of Mr. Teufel's books lying around: Father had given me one of them as a Christmas gift the previous December, when, upon returning home from the City for winter break, I had mentioned a few details of my run-in with the writer at Hollow Hills.

It was 5 o'clock in the evening by the time I left Karswell Hall. I headed west until I had reached the big gates that served as the main entrance onto the campus, the gates that bore an uncanny similarity to Rodin's *The Gates of Hell* sculpture. I passed through these gates and stepped onto Fludd Street, which was the street where the university was located (I neglected to mention it before, but the name of the college I went to was Fludd University). I then began walking south, in the direction of the park. It was still light out, a mildly warm May day, to the extent that I didn't need to wear a coat at all. That evening I was wearing my usual ensemble of tight black leather pants and ratty black Dr. Martens boots, while for a shirt I had on a white short-sleeved t-shirt, on the front of which was an iconic 1974 Frank Stefanko photograph of the impossibly thin punk rocker Patti Smith (herself clad in a Keith Richards t-shirt) black hair cut short and uncombed, with her left hand posed provocatively on her hip and right hand holding a cigarette (or maybe it was a marijuana joint, I'm not really sure). The epitome of sexy squalor in a manner of speaking, but then again, I've always found 1970's-era Patti Smith something of a turn-on, though my ultimate crush is still 1980's-era Lydia Lunch (the first woman I ever had an orgasm over, FYI). I had my black iPod clipped to my pants and my earbuds were in place, and as I walked the few blocks to the bookstore I was listening to the 1960 Elvis Presley song 'Black Star', which was actually the only Elvis song I had saved to my iPod library. I wasn't a big fan of his work by any stretch of the imagination but I had come to enjoy this particular song ever since I had read on the internet that it was supposedly an influence on *Blackstar*, the final David Bowie album (I had gotten this Elvis song from my friend George, who was an Elvis fanatic and pretty much owned CDs of every one of the King's albums: George himself had a room at Karswell Hall, just down the hall from the room that Dinah and I shared). As I made my way to Covers, I softly hummed along to the song.

Once I had reached the northeast perimeter of the park I took a right and stepped onto Bastion Street. I then walked along the black wrought-iron fence that lined the northern perimeter of the park until I arrived at the block that Covers was located on. The bookstore was easy to spot from a distance as a long line of people were patiently lined up outside its front entrance, no doubt waiting for Mr. Teufel's book signing to start. I don't have much to say about the exterior of Covers: architecturally speaking it was painfully generic, as dull and devoid of interest as a Maroon 5 album. Dinah usually shunned the establishment as she deemed it "way too corporate" (in contrast to the hip and funky independent antiquarian bookstores we more commonly frequented), but I didn't really mind the place; at the very least, the staff was pleasant and knowledgeable. Once I had arrived outside of the bookstore, I took a place at the very end of the line. Aside from my iPod, all I had with me on my person that evening was my black purse, inside of which was my copy of *Sex and Violets*, which was the first short story collection written by Hector Teufel, and published by Viking in 1986: the front cover showcased a lurid painting of that leering hobgoblin known as Puck.

The event was set to begin at 5:30, and sure enough, when that time rolled around the staff of Covers opened up the doors and the line of people began to slowly be sucked into the store: to my overactive imagination, I pictured all of us as ants sliding down the tongue of some gargantuan anteater. A few minutes later and I had passed the threshold of the doors and now found myself standing inside the bookstore. The interior of Covers was just about as banal as its exterior: aside from the stacks of books, it was mainly just lots of oak furniture and wood paneling, elegant portraits of famous writers lining the walls, the smell of fatty food and fresh coffee wafting from the store's

Starbucks café like a billowing cloud of toxic gas, giant posters depicting cover artwork of novels like *1984*, *Brave New World*, and so on. Music was playing softly over the store's sound system, 'Men in a War' by Suzanne Vega (from her underrated 1990 art-rock album *Days of Open Hand*), and that was one consolation: at least the music they were playing didn't suck.

I switched off my iPod, then took off my earbuds and let them dangle around my neck as I waited patiently in line. This line was slowly moving towards the center of the store, in the direction of the main aisle that ran from the front entrance to the children's department in back. In the center of the main aisle, I could see that a table had been set up, and this table was where the signing itself was taking place. As I slowly moved closer and closer to this table, I could see that its surface was covered with stacks of books, these books being the new novel written by Hector Teufel: *Jacob's Triumph*. The front cover of the book was adorned with Gustave Doré's famous 1855 engraving *Jacob Wrestling with the Angel*. I had absolutely zero intention of buying this new book of his, having no interest in Christian Fiction at all, so instead I took out my own copy of *Sex and Violets* with the notion of getting him to sign that for me. I didn't really have any great desire to get his autograph: this was all just an excuse to see him up close.

Eventually there was only one person in front of me in the line, and now I had a much better view of Mr. Teufel. Physically, he still looked much as he had the first night we had met, though he was now more smartly dressed, and no longer seemed as if he were down and out in Heaven and Hell. To my great shock, he was all but radiating a halo of goodwill. As he finished signing the book of the person in front of me, I stepped forward, book in hand. For a second our eyes met, and looking into those eyes was like being stranded in the icy wastes of some Mountains of Madness. They were the one thing that gave away the illusion he was trying to create, for in those orbs I saw no metaphorical soaring golden chariots of angelic ambition: instead I saw the sinister sneakiness of black helicopters. I looked for a spark of recognition in those frozen and oversized eyes of his, but could find nothing … had he forgotten about me that quickly?

After exchanging the usual banal pleasantries, he took the proffered book from me (taking a moment as he did so to compliment me for owning one of his lesser-known works), and asked me to whom he should sign the book to. In the meanwhile, 'The Attack of the Killer Ants' by Blondie had begun to play in the background, which made the following brief conversation somewhat disorientating.

"You really don't remember me, do you?" I asked. I was trying to project a too-cool-for-school façade, but in truth my throat was as dry as the Atacama Desert in South America (which, according to Wikipedia, is the driest place on earth).

Mr. Teufel looked into my eyes again, this time seeming to notice me for real. "You do look familiar," he said, in a voice that suggested that he was in deep contemplation on the matter. "Wait, now I remember you … that bartender at Hollow Hills. Hamsa Cauldron, right?"

"So you *do* remember me," I said. "We had quite the odd conversation, you and I. At the time, you seemed to be in something of a fallow state of mind, but it seems as if you're doing quite well now."

"What can I say?" Mr. Teufel asked, practically beaming. "I found myself a new muse. Ah, Hamsa, if only you could see her! She's so very beautiful … *divinely* beautiful, one could claim. Such an improvement over my old murdered muse, to be sure. I have her to thank for my reinvention as a writer, for the rejuvenation of my stalled literary career."

I felt a little miffed by that latter claim of his: after all, as far as I could recall it had been *my* suggestion that he should try to reinvent himself, but I decided to let it go. "You seem … different," I eventually said, unsure of what else to say to him.

"Finding religion can be a bracing tonic. Since we last spoke, I have been washed anew in the Blood of the Lamb, and all of my sins have been forgiven. Hallelujah!" Mr. Teufel exclaimed cheerfully, his gaze briefly rolling up to stare at the heavens.

By this point in our conversation, I was worried that he might try and convert me, then and there; it seemed as if he still had his old zeal for sermonizing. Luckily, I began to feel impatient vibes from the person standing in line behind me. Mr. Teufel obviously picked up on these vibes as well, for he promptly signed my copy of *Sex and Violets*, wished me the best of luck for my own writing career, then sent me on my way with a hearty "God Bless!"

Not having any good reason to remain in the bookstore now that my mission was accomplished, I left the establishment. Still feeling flummoxed by this unexpected encounter, I crossed the street and walked over to the coffee shop, which was directly across from Covers. I entered the coffeehouse, where I stopped just inside the main entrance to get a bearing on my new surroundings. The place was all but deserted at that hour, save for a few economic majors from the university, all of whom were flipping through Thomas Piketty's *Capitalism in the Twenty-First Century* in a desultory manner (and really, who could blame them?). Music was playing over the café's internal sound system, and I recognized the tune: 'When the World Was at War We Kept Dancing' by Lana Del Rey. I sauntered over to the barista behind the counter and ordered a café latte. Once I had been served, I took my drink from her and took a seat at a round wooden table near the front of the store, right by a big square window that gave me a good view of the Covers bookstore I had vacated mere moments before. Slowly sipping my drink, I watched as the business there slowly died down By seven o'clock, the signing had ended and the store had closed up for the night. One of the last people to leave (not counting the staff) was Mr. Teufel. I watched as he slunk off into the night, in a manner that seemed highly suspicious to me. Still curious about his unexpected transformation, and wondering just what he was up to, I resolved to follow him for the purposes of my own enlightenment. So I rose from my seat, left a few crumpled bills on the surface of the table by way of a generous tip (and why not? The barista was hot, in a 'Miley Cyrus wearing a red 'make America gay again' baseball hat' kind of way), then exited the coffeehouse.

Standing in the night air outside the coffee house, I looked down Bastion Street, to the west, which was the direction that Mr. Teufel had seemed to be heading in. From my vantage point, I could see him walking away in the distance, his back to me. I began to follow him, sticking to the shadows and keeping my distance so that he wouldn't spot me, and feeling like a private eye or an 8-eyed spy as I did so … luckily, he seemed distracted by his own thoughts.

By now night had well and truly fallen over the City, though it could be argued that night hadn't merely descended, rather that it *blossomed* in the sky, as if the very atmosphere had been tainted by some Satanic chrism. I could see that it was a full moon out, and one long stray worm-like cloud seemed to be attached to the Moon's eastern side, causing the celestial body to resemble (to my eyes at least) an enormous spermatozoon as conceptualized by Victorian scientific illustrators. Even something about the stars seemed wrong: that evening they struck me as being less harmonious luminous spheres of gas and more like the pulverized remnants of some long-forgotten Titanomachy. Staring up at the stars and the Moon caused me to briefly neglect my task: I found myself wondering if perhaps the night sky was nothing more than a giant mirror crafted by unknown hands, a cosmic looking glass whose sole purpose was to reflect our own spiritual emptiness back at us. Then I remembered that I was supposed to be following Mr. Teufel, so I returned to my quest. I wasn't quite sure what the point of this quest even was, yet I felt compelled to follow him through the twilight, as if he were a sorcerer who had enchanted me with some diabolical geas.

The two of us continued walking down Bastion Street, until I spotted Mr. Teufel taking a left and heading down Short Street. I followed him, and soon on my right side I was passing by the Phantom Films Movie Palace: letters on the marquee above the front doors informed me that the theater was holding a Michael Reeves double-bill feature that night, the films in question being *The Sorcerers* and *Conqueror Worm*. After passing by the Phantom Films Movie Palace, Mr. Teufel and I stepped onto Stream Street. Here, Mr. Teufel turned to his right and continued heading west. Stream Street was a very long street that stretched out along the entire southern border of the City, and it was so named because it also ran along the border of the river (though technically speaking, it probably should have been named River Street). Even though Mr. Teufel still seemed to be preoccupied with his own inner thoughts, I began acting a bit more cautious at this juncture of our journey across the night lands of the City, for this street was somewhat better illuminated than the one we had just left. Sometimes, when he passed beneath a streetlight, I could see his shadow trailing on the street behind him, an oddly apish shape that made me once again think of the weird-looking beast on the cover art of that old Fleetwood Mac LP *Mystery To Me*, which caused me to wonder if Mr. Teufel had ever really lost his muse in the first place: that all this time he had been searching for it had been a waste, for all he ever had to do was simply look behind him, and there it was. And I know what some people who are reading this narrative might now be thinking: how is it that a black 19 year-old Goth girl knows so much about Fleetwood Mac? Well, to those skeptical souls I would say that it just so happened that Father has been a lifelong fan of Fleetwood

Mac and plays those albums all of the time, hence my familiarity with them (apropos of nothing, he also had a huge crush on Stevie Nicks, who he thought was not only the best female singer of all-time, but also quite possibly the most beautiful woman of all, and there are days where I think he may be right).

It would be remiss of me to neglect to mention here that Stream Street was one of the City's more scenic avenues, and we passed by a number of interesting buildings and landmarks on our way to wherever it was that Mr. Teufel was heading. To provide just a few examples, on the other side of the street (and not far from the banks of the river), there was a large fish statue that bore a singular resemblance to the one that appears in the central panel on the third page of the 17th issue of Neil Gaiman's *The Sandman* comic book (the name of that issue being 'Calliope'). We also passed by the towering Pyramid Bank, which was easily the tallest building in the entire City: it looked like a long and narrow 28-story pyramid, one made of featureless black marble, undecorated by even a single window. Pyramid Bank was actually a great source of gossip among the university's more paranoid and conspiracy theory-obsessed students, as there were rumors that the building was owned by a shadowy company that practiced obscure rites in honor of the deities Qioxtl and Yxthahl.

At one point during our voyage I could see, across the river, St. Drogo's Cathedral (St. Drogo being the patron saint of ugly people), this church bearing a strong likeness to the old St. John's Roman Catholic Church that one could find existing at Atwells Avenue in Providence, Rhode Island, once upon a time (that is, until it was torn down in 1992); most likely this was because the two churches had both been designed by the same man, James Murphy. Or rather I should say that St. Drogo's *used* to resemble that church in Providence, for that evening St. Drogo's Cathedral had burst into flames, a holocaust of fire that seemed to make a very mockery of the attempts made by the City's firemen to extinguish it. I took a brief moment to watch the burning cathedral, and while I felt bad to see such a beautiful-looking building reduced to ashes, there was something undoubtedly hypnotic about the way that the flames were arcing through the night sky. One of the blazing steeples even, for one hallucinatory minute, seemed to resemble the head, mane and neck of some great and terrible horse made of flames: an Equine of the Inferno, the steed of the unknown Fifth Horsemen of the Apocalypse: the Horseman of Conflagration.

Finally, Mr. Teufel came to a stop outside a derelict-looking bungalow house near the southwest corner of the City's western border, near the corner of Spectral Street. Here he paused to look both ways up and down the street, so as to be sure that no one was observing him (by this point I had ducked into the shadows of a nearby alleyway to avoid being spotted, so he didn't see me). Once he had evidently satisfied himself that he wasn't being followed, he entered the building.

For a few minutes I waited in the relative safety of my hiding place, unsure as to what my next move should be. Finally, I stepped out of the alleyway and walked over to the front lawn of the bungalow house, a lawn that was overgrown with weeds. Now that I stood directly in front of the building, I had a better view of its architectural charms, which were practically nihil. It was pretty much a textbook example of the bungalow house as a concept, in that it was a mostly horizontal one story structure with a low-pitched roof and broad eaves, with a sizeable front porch. There was, however, one aspect of the house that struck me as most curious. It was that the front entrance leading into the house was lacking a door: it was as if the bungalow was inviting any and all to enter it, much like the sinister House of Silence that appears in William Hope Hodgson's *The Night Land*. If this place was indeed Mr. Teufel's current place of address, it was certainly a most bizarre one, though perhaps I shouldn't have been all that surprised.

Obviously I had no intention of entering the house while Mr. Teufel remained inside it. Instead I snuck around to the western side of the building and peeked into one of the windows, which let me see into the living room at the front of the house. This living room was all but devoid of furniture, though in the center of the room someone had set up a Crux decussata, or St. Andrew's Cross. Commonly found in BDSM dungeons, this one was of the typical x-shape of such things, and someone (or perhaps I should say something) was chained to the Cross by its ankles and wrists, forcing it to assume a spread eagled position (with its back against the wood of the Cross). The being chained to the Cross was an angel, and I mean that in the most literal sense of the word. This angel was naked and utterly genderless, having no sexual organs to speak of. Sprouting from its back were two enormous feathery wings marked with hundreds of dazzling and exotic peacock eyes, while its head was not that of a human but instead a regal-looking predatory bird, which instantly made me think of the rooster-headed Abraxas of the Gnostics, and also Loplop, the avian alter ego of the Surrealist artist Max Ernst. Its naked body was also covered with fine markings, but I was too far away to be able to make out just what those markings were, as the room was somewhat poorly lit, the only illumination coming from a fire blazing away inside a fireplace in one of the room's corners: sparks were bursting forth from the burning log, briefly rising into the air before plummeting back to earth, like a multitude of miniature phoenixes that had been reborn, only to change their mind and fall back down to the Inferno beneath them, eager to return to the cold tendrils of death and non-existence

Hector Teufel was standing before this anguiped angel, with a razor in one hand and a small grail held in the other. He was engaged in a one-sided conversation with the celestial being, and the walls of the bungalow house were thin enough so that I could pretty much hear every word he spoke.

"Good evening, my dear," he all but purred to the captive angel. "You're looking as splendid as always, I must say. Well, considering your present circumstances and all. I apologize again for the desuetude of your surroundings. Now that money is no longer an issue for me I really must spruce this place up a bit one day. Anyway, you can probably gather why I'm here. I've come to make the usual small withdrawal. Come now, no need to flinch and thrash about so, it's very unbecoming. It'll only pinch a little, and I assure you that not a single drop shall go to waste."

After this brief spiel had concluded, Mr. Teufel stepped forward, razor and grail still in hand. I watched spellbound as he used the razor to make a small incision on the angel's left breast. Almost instantly white blood began to fountain out, which Mr. Teufel collected with his grail. Once the grail was full, he pressed a handkerchief up against the cut he had made until it had formed a scar which no longer bled. He then took a sip from the grail and, closing his eyes, smiled.

"There, that wasn't so bad now, was it? I told you it wouldn't hurt that much," Mr. Teufel told his prisoner. "There's no need to cry, though. I know you must think of me as cruel, and I really wish there was some other way, but sadly, there isn't. Please don't think of me as an ungrateful bastard … I really do appreciate the gifts I've taken from you. Well … I should be headed back home now, it's been a long day. Until next time, my dear … I'll see you soon."

Mr. Teufel placed the razor down on the dusty surface of a table located near the main entrance. Still holding the now-full grail, he turned and exited the bungalow house, walking slowly now to avoid spilling a single drop. I peered around the side of the house and watched as he began heading back the way we had come, now heading east. I watched as he grew smaller and smaller the further he walked away, and a few seconds later he had vanished from sight entirely. Once I was certain that he had left for good, I walked around the side of the house and ascended the creaking porch steps, until I stood before the entrance that was devoid of a door. Taking a deep breath, I then entered Mr. Teufel's bungalow house.

Once inside, I picked up the razor and walked towards the pinioned angel, who was still in the act of weeping, and thus unaware of my presence. Now that I was closer to it, I could see that the fine lines that adorned its body were in fact scars, dozens upon dozens of them, no doubt inflicted by Mr. Teufel's greedy razor, its once immaculate body reduced to crimson king ruin. It was as if its *anima mundi* (or world-soul) had become irrevocably tainted by some insidious malison: this was paradise lost, the Nightside of Eden, Arcadia mutated into the Venomenon (a Plane of Cosmic Horror). As I stared at the angel, I was all but hypnotized by its ethereal beauty, and how it managed to project an air of exalted dignity, in spite of its very undignified circumstances.

Gradually, the angel's weeping trailed away, and it slowly came to realize that a stranger now stood before it. Our eyes met, and for a second neither of us said a word. And then, upon noticing the razor in my hand, it said, in a whispery voice, "Please … release me."

And for a hair's breadth that was exactly what I had planned on doing: using the razor to cut away the ropes that held its hands and feet in place. I wanted to watch it hobble out of that awful bungalow house, unfurl its beautiful wings, and fly back to its rightful place in the western welkin above. But before I could act on that noble impulse, I remembered that I also had that creative writing paper due next week, and still no ideas as to what I would write about. "I'm sorry," I muttered, as I used the razor to make a small cut in the angel's chest, not that far from the most recent cut that Mr. Teufel had made. I watched in amazement as blood that was as white as milk began to seep from the wound. I dropped the razor and fell to my knees and raised my head and opened my mouth and let the angel's blood flow down my throat.

As I greedily swallowed the white blood guzzling from the wound of the weeping angel, and as I could literally feel the ideas for a short story blooming in my mind, I realized that it was quite a shame that Hector Teufel couldn't see me now; no doubt he'd be nodding his head in grim approval, a Mephistophelian smile in place on his face, happy to see that I was well on my way to embarking on a successful literary career.